She's My Sister
The Comfort Tree

By Kevin P. DuBois

Illustrated by Elif Balta Parks

ISBN: 978-1-954614-23-9 (hard cover)
      978-1-954614-24-6 (soft cover)

Editing: Amy Ashby

Published by Warren Publishing
Charlotte, NC
www.warrenpublishing.net
Printed in the United States

*Dedicated to my wife, my forever companion
on this SMS journey. To my oldest daughter,
who loves her baby sister and is wise beyond
her years, and to my youngest daughter, who
continues to tackle milestones as she manages
life with Smith-Magenis Syndrome (SMS).*

She's my sister, the one over there,
quietly twirling her light blonde hair.
Just three years old, my best friend from the start,
providing laughter and letting me share my heart.

She's yet to say a word, but she understands what I say,
following me around the house, signing for me to play.
At times she gets frustrated, but I've learned to embrace
any chance to distract her and put a smile on her face.

My name is Nora, my sister's very best friend,
we do everything together, but we're best at playing pretend.
Pretending we are princesses, pretending to be vets,
lying on the bean bag as we "pretend" to rest.

I would do anything for her, she's everything to me;
I love making her laugh and pointing out things I see:
a bird atop a nest, squawking music through the air;
our schnauzers running briskly, catching the wind in their hair.

It's the little things for me, like a plant growing from a seed,
sharing my life with my sister is all I really need.
So no one has to remind me, it's something I want to do;
keeping an eye on my sister is really nothing new.

I love looking after her, it comes naturally to me.
No matter the situation, I am her comfort tree.
A place for my sister to relax and rest her head,
a place of calm before she heads off to bed.

At times I notice she gets shy and hides,
walks away from people, with me close to her side.
The noise may be too loud, shrinking the room in space,
but as long as she can spot me, calmness fills her face.

I reach out my hand and take hers in mine,
never forgetting we're sisters, locked together in time.
No words can describe how important to me
it is for my sister to lean on her comfort tree.

As the sun sets on my day, I dream of paths to take,
ways to help my sister find a new landscape.
I know it's out there, a place where we can go
to relieve her frustrations and allow her smile to grow.

Before I shut my eyes, I look to the sky,
make one last wish and help my sister fly
to a place far away, a place as pretty as her,
a sanctuary of calm, with a map as our chauffeur.

The morning sun awakens and shines into my room,
waking me up as my day begins to bloom.
At the end of the bed sits a sparkly new box!
It's inscribed with my name and has no ties or locks.

I carefully walk over and open it for a peek.
A note sits on top, stating, "This is the wish you seek.
Each map in this box will take you from this place,
guide you on an adventure, where frustrations are erased.

"When you call out,
the maps will appear;
they can only be used
when the intent is clear.
I'll listen for your voice,
and if the moment is right,
a map will unravel,
and your journey will take flight.

"There's only one rule
and it is very simple,
(your request for the maps
comes with a wrinkle).
You can only ask
when a map is truly needed.
If you disregard this rule,
your maps will be depleted!

"When you are ready, call for the maps;
just shout my name, they'll arrive in a snap.
It's easy to remember and easy to say;
the name you must call out is 'Miss Getaway.'"

Not knowing what to do, I pause and take another read;
could this be a blessing, everything my sister needs?
A quick way to disappear when she's getting mad,
a place to make her happy when she's feeling sad?

She's my sister, the one over there,
with her pink little glasses and skin that's fair.
The voyages we'll take, the journeys we'll travel,
nothing to stop us, just maps to unravel.

My name is Nora, and it's plain to see
I'll always have my sister,
and she'll have her comfort tree.
I've been delivered a way
to quickly take her to places,
disappear for a while,
leaving only magical dust traces ... .